To Katrina

L W Lewis

D1074471

Poodles, Tigers, Monsters & You

L.W. Lewis

Artwork by
Lorrayne R. Harris

Red Pumpkin Press
Bluffton, SC

Copyright © 2004, Red Pumpkin Press
ISBN: 0-9711572-1-9
LCCN: 2004096137

For my grandchildren

Kyle

Mitch

Clara

Jimmy

ORDER BOOKS FOR FRIENDS AND RELATIVES
(Makes a Great Birthday Gift)
Cut out order form and send to:
L.W. Lewis
4 Cheswell Ct.
Bluffton, SC 29909

Your Name _____

Address _____

_____

City _____ ST _____ ZIP _____

	Cost		Quantity		Total
Poodles, Tigers, Monsters, & You	12.95	x	_____	=	_____
Why Do Flies Eat Doggy Poop	14.95	x	_____	=	_____
				Grand Total	_____

Make check or money order payable to L.W. Lewis

SHIPPING IS FREE!

Poodles, Tigers, Monsters & You

IF A POODLE MARRIED A TIGER

If a poodle married a tiger
And they had a little child,
Would it be warm and cuddly
Or would it be mean and wild?

Something very loving,
That licks you on the nose,
Or maybe something dangerous
That tries to bite your toes?

And if you were its master,
Would it consider you a winner,
Or maybe take a different view,
And think of you as dinner?

I wouldn't want to own that pet.
I think it would be too scary.
And that's probably the major reason,
Poodles and tigers never marry.

A MONSTER'S BIRTHDAY PARTY

I got invited to a monster's birthday party.
I hate to say, "I was very tardy."
More than tardy, I'd call it slow.
To tell the truth, I didn't go.

He was a monster I hardly knew.
His teeth are green and his fur is blue.
His face is white with a yellow snoot.
As monsters go, he's kind of cute.

So I phoned the monster's house to see,
Just why the monster had invited me,
And what they planned on doing there,
And about the clothes that I should wear.

He said don't worry about your clothes,
Just shove raisins up your nose.
Put lemon pudding on both your knees,
Wear lots of honey from honeybees.

Wear chocolate sprinkles in your hair,
With strawberry syrup everywhere.
And please don't wear a coat or shirt,
Because you've been invited as dessert.

BATHING KITTY

I bathed our kitten and she's squeaky clean,
But now she's afraid of the washing machine.
She's been crying and meowing. I think it's stress.
But I used gentle cycle and permanent press.

At first she swam, but a short time later,
She got too close to the agitator.
I tried to grab her, but she was out of reach,
So all I could do was add more bleach.

Cats hate soapy water, so it's hard to win.
But mine wasn't happy with rinse or spin.
So I took her out early when she started to cry.
I thought she'd feel better if she could tumble dry.

So how do you keep an animal clean?
I love my kitten. I don't want to be mean.
I'm sure I made a big mistake.
I should not have washed her—with my snake.

THE QUESTION

I'd like to ask a question,
About a bug that's hairy and green.
Do you think he's just a nuisance,
Or could he be dangerous and mean?

Could he be full of venom,
And sting just like an ant?
Or is he a lot more gentle,
And will only eat a plant?

Perhaps it's not important.
You may not even care.
But I think that I should tell you,
I see him crawling in your hair.

ON PICKING A PET

I wouldn't want to have
A spider for a pet.
Spiders are as scary
As anything can get.

And frogs are very slimy,
They wiggle and they're icky.
And if you let one kiss you,
Its tongue is really sticky.

And it sure doesn't take a wizard
To know you wouldn't want a lizard.
They have way too many scales.
Besides, their bodies are mostly tails.

But those are my only choices,
I have to pick one or another.
So I guess my parents are right,
We're keeping my newborn brother.

NO UNDERWEAR

Oh my gosh! I do declare!
I forgot to put on underwear!
The playground is where I want to go,
But if I do my rear will show.

Hopscotch is what I want to play
But I'll have to pass that up today.
I like the slide, but you know what?
Kids would laugh if they saw my butt.

I'm missing the fun and it's not fair.
I tried to get some underwear.
I phoned my mom, but I can't reach her.
I can't leave class, because I'm the teacher.

AUNT ELIZABETH

Daddy has a half-sister.
I don't know which half it is.
But I think I know her half-name,
Because Daddy calls her Liz

I'm not sure if he's the brother
Of her bottom or her top.
Or how the line is drawn,
Or where it'd start or stop.

Perhaps he's just related
To her hands but not her feet.
Or maybe left and right
Is how the two halves meet.

I may never figure out
Just where the division is.
But it really doesn't matter,
Because I love all of Auntie Liz!

MY NEW PET

My father said I could pick a pet,
So I plan to have the best one yet.
I don't want a dog or cat,
I think I'd soon get bored with that.

I want something that's handy with a mop and a broom,
A pet that will help me clean my room,
One who likes to pat me on the head,
Pick up my toys and make my bed.

And another thing that effects my decision,
How good is it at long division?
While I am outside having fun,
Will all my homework be getting done?

And on days when I am blue or sad
Will my pet do things to make me glad?
Like read a book, or watch TV,
Or maybe bake a cake for me.

But Daddy said I can't have that pet,
That I'll have to pick another.
He said the pet I want to own
Just happens to be my mother.

ETIQUETTE

Etiquette is how to eat,
The proper way to cut your meat.
There are many rules in etiquette books,
But it's a lot easier than it looks.

Never shove noodles up your nose.
Don't wrap spaghetti between your toes.
You don't eat soup with a knife and fork.
And don't put mud on beef or pork.

Mashed potatoes don't go on your head.
Never eat chicken if it's not dead.
You don't eat dinner standing up.
And don't blow bubbles in your cup.

Go to restaurants wearing clothes.
Never use a napkin to blow your nose.
Close your mouth each time you chew.
And don't let gravy spill on you.

I did not become this well bred,
From anything I studied or read.
Just common sense was all it took.
I've never read an etiquette book.

MY BARBIE

I got a brand new Barbie,
And she is truly great.
I call her Skater Barbie
When she twirls a figure eight.

She can even go in water.
She's nice and trim and slim.
I call her Swimmer Barbie
When I take her for a swim.

And she has pretty dresses,
She loves to skip and prance.
So I call her Barbie Dancer,
When I take her to a dance.

But my brother played with matches.
And by the time that he was through,
I had to change my dolly's name,
Now I call her "Barbie-Que."

College

If it's about going to college,
I've made my final decision.
I'm not going to Harvard,
Because they do long division.

They don't even divide by a number,
They divide by a number square.
So I'm not going to Harvard,
They'll make me do that there.

I'm already taking English,
I'm learning how to spell.
And every day in pre-school
I do Play-Doh really well.

But if they make me do long division,
There is a good chance I could fail.
So I'm not going to Harvard.
I'll probably go to Yale!

WHY FROGS ARE GREEN

I think I know why frogs are green,
They eat the worse things that I've ever seen.
It shouldn't come as a big surprise,
Wouldn't you turn green, if you ate flies?

If every time you wanted a treat,
All you got were bugs to eat.
I don't think it would be much of a joke,
As a matter-of-fact, you might even croak.

NEVER INVITE A MONSTER TO DINNER

I invited a monster to dinner.
He got fat and I got thinner.
While I was cooking he didn't wait,
He ate his fork and he ate his plate.

I wanted to sit, but we weren't able,
He'd eaten both the chairs and table.
He ate the ham and two cherry pies,
All the salad and all the fries.

We went to the couch to sit and chat,
But it was gone, he'd eaten that.
He ate my rug and TV set.
And I believe he ate more yet.

I can't prove it, but I'm pretty certain,
That he's the one who ate my curtain.
He probably ate my baseball bat,
And I still can't find my dog or cat.

OUTSIDE NAKED

My little brother's outside naked,
He's not wearing any clothes.
He's splashing in a puddle,
There's mud between his toes.

He's jumping and he's running,
A happy little guy.
Pushing our red sailboat,
There's a twinkle in his eye.

He's laughing and he's joyful,
I see a smile upon his face.
If I were five years younger,
Then I could take his place.

But that isn't going to happen,
It's just not meant to be.
He's only twenty-seven,
While I'm already thirty-three.

TOMMY

Tommy is pretty much older than me.
He's already five, while I'm just three.
But I don't think that Tommy's so smart,
When kindergarten opened, he didn't start.

Tommy doesn't know the alphabet,
And Tommy can't really speak well yet.
But we watch television every day,
Then Tommy and I go outside and play.

For three full years our friendship's grown.
He's always with me. I'm never alone.
And there's no one else can take his place,
Especially, when he wags his tail, or licks my face.

THE DREAM

We all had an argument.
Who had the strangest dream?
Bobby was in the navy,
He commanded a submarine.

Donna was in a forest
Where she met a talking bear.
But he wasn't mean or dangerous,
In fact, he combed her hair.

Wanda rode on a spaceship.
She took a trip to Mars,
And met two purple Martians
Who were driving fancy cars.

But my dream was the strangest
Any of us had ever seen,
We walked into my bedroom,
And everything was clean!

IF I WERE A TREE

If I were a tree,
I'd wear a hat.
And most of my branches
Would be a bat.

I'd make friends
With the birds and bees,
And I'd play ball
With the other trees.

We would all grow
In just the right places.
And we'd ask the squirrels
To run the bases.

On each baseline
Would be a wise old owl.
And he would decide
What is fair or foul.

And way high up
In the tallest tree,
There would be
An umpire bee.

He'd call the squirrels
Either safe or out.
While all the flowers
Would cheer and shout.

Of all the trees
There could ever be,
Like maple, oak,
Or mahogany.

There is only one
That appeals to me.
I'd like to be
A baseball tree.

THE DERRIERE

Mother said if I don't act nicer,
She's going to spank my derriere.
So I'm pretty sure I've got one,
But I have no idea where.

It isn't in my closet,
Because I looked up on the shelf.
And I don't think it's something,
I can find all by myself.

So I got my dog to help me;
He found my bat and ball.
We searched for over an hour,
But no derriere at all.

We looked all through the kitchen.
We made a great big mess.
We even went in Mother's room
And pulled down her best dress.

Mother couldn't even find it.
She didn't do what she had said.
She didn't spank my derriere,
She spanked my butt instead.

I HATE TO LOSE

I like to win
But I hate to lose.
I scream a lot
And throw my shoes.

I haven't lost in quite awhile,
Not because I've got great style.
I haven't lost to a he or she,
Because no one wants to play with me.

A BOY'S GARDEN

I wish flowers could run around
Instead of growing in the ground.
You can't play ball with a rose or fern,
But it would be fun if they could learn.

If a daffodil could swing a bat
And dandelions wore a glove and hat.
If a petunia was able to drop a bunt
Or a violet knew how to pass or punt.

If a gardenia was able to hit-and-run,
Or a zinnia thought that pitching was fun.
If a marigold could steal a base,
A garden would be a wonderful place!

THE SNOWMAN

My cousin made a snowman.
He built him out of sticks.
My brother made a stronger one,
He built him out of bricks.

My sister cooked a little one.
He's made from cookie dough.
But I like mine the very best,
Because I made him out of snow.

MY MOTHER

My mother is such a monster,
Her feet are even hairy.
All of her teeth are snaggled
And her voice is really scary.

Her hands are dark and wrinkled,
On her fingers she has claws.
I'm not sure they are really hands,
Perhaps they might be paws.

Her eyes are small and red.
They glow when it gets dark,
So I can always find her
When she takes me to the park.

Her stomach sticks way out.
Her fur is orange and blue.
And I think that she's so beautiful,
Because I'm a monster too.

ANOTHER SISTER

If he had another sister,
There's no way that she could be
Any nicer to him,
Or prettier than me.

If he had another sister
She wouldn't be as smart,
She couldn't be as charming,
Or have a better heart.

If he had another sister,
I don't think that he would find,
That she would be as honest,
Or even half as kind.

But if I had another brother,
He wouldn't be a brat.
And if he hid my dolly,
He'd show me where it's at.

MONSTERS

Do monsters think other monsters are beautiful?
Do they ever go out on a date?
Do girl monsters wear short skirts and makeup?
And do they make their boyfriends wait?

Do they ever get starry-eyed and dreamy,
Or walk through the park claw-in-claw?
Are sharp fangs and bad breath attractive,
Or is it still considered a flaw?

Do monsters ever give flowers?
Do they ever have a best friend?
Do they ever write cards or letters,
When monsters have love to send?

Do monsters blow kisses and smile?
Do they ever give away their heart?
Well, if they do, maybe monsters are human,
Or at least that's a pretty good start.

THE LION AND THE ZEBRA

The lion and the zebra got married,
And the wedding turned out fine.
But they weren't married very long—
Only until dinnertime.

MY JOB

When I grow up and start working,
I know what I want to be.
I've thought a lot about it.
The job that is right for me.

More fun than a baseball player,
Even better than an astronaut,
I'm not going to be a doctor,
But I will love my job a lot.

My job will be important,
Just like a movie star.
I'll make a lot of money,
And I'll drive a fancy car.

My job will be the greatest,
Better than any other.
Because what I'd really like to be,
Is the boss of my older brother.

MY WEIGHT

I wouldn't say I'm fat.
I don't weigh that much.
I'm maybe a little heavy,
But only just a touch.

There are lots of other things
That weigh much more than me,
A walrus and an elephant,
A polar bear and redwood tree.

Compared to all those other things,
My weight is lighter than it sounds.
I got on the scale yesterday -
I'm just six-hundred thirty pounds.

PLAYING WITH MY NEWBORN SISTER

Can I please play with my newborn sister?
Because yesterday I really missed her.
I was playing baseball, catching flys,
Talking about her to the other guys.

I know she's small and can't move around,
But she could lie there on the ground.
Her blanket would protect her face,
And we need to use her—as second base.

SALAD

I don't think that argument is valid.
I won't get bigger if I eat salad.
Mommy eats salad and she's still small.
Whales never eat any salad at all.

I'm not very fond of lettuce and such.
And I don't like tomatoes that much.
I don't consider parsley a treat.
And even worse is a pickled beet.

So don't get mad if I don't eat greens.
It's not my fault that I don't like beans.
But I'll get big and I'll tell you why,
I like to eat lots of cake and pie.

MY DOGGY HAS NO TAIL

My doggy has no tail,
That's what people say.
But he doesn't need a tail,
To go outside and play.

It's true he has no tail,
Not even a little bit.
But what dog needs a tail,
Just to run and play and sit.

And if he has no tail,
Why should I even care?
He's such a special doggy,
With lots of love to share.

So how do I know he loves me?
That crazy little mutt.
It's true, he can't wag his tail,
But he sure can wag his butt.

MY SISTER

My sister won't climb on rocks or logs.
She's afraid of bugs and pollywogs.
She's terrified of a snake or a mouse.
She screams if a spider gets in the house.

She won't pet dogs any bigger than a cat.
She's afraid of the sun so she wears a hat.
She won't play ball because she'll break a nail.
She does her homework; she's afraid she'll fail.

Afraid of everything under the sun,
My sister's really not much fun.
Afraid of things she can't even see,
So why is she not afraid of me?

WALTER JOHNSON

I hate that Walter Johnson.
His toes are really fat,
He gets bad grades in school,
And it smells bad where he sat.

I really hate Walter Johnson.
His glasses are very nerdy,
He makes disgusting noises,
And his shoes are always dirty.

I hate, hate, hate Walter Johnson.
It's the way he parts his hair,
How he zips his zipper,
And the clothes he likes to wear.

Oh, how I hate Walter Johnson.
I might even hate his mom.
But what I hate the most about him,
He didn't invite me to the prom.

THE PURPLE FISH

I wish I had a purple fish
And that his fins were green.
I'd like him to be friendly,
Not sarcastic, rude, or mean.

I wish that he could read to me,
And maybe sing a little song,
Then help me with my homework,
Just the problems I get wrong.

Perhaps he could play the violin,
Or even knit a sweater.
And if he helped me with my room,
I'd like him even better.

I wish that he were in a race
And that he was the winner.
Then I'd take my purple fishy home,
And I'd fry him up for dinner.

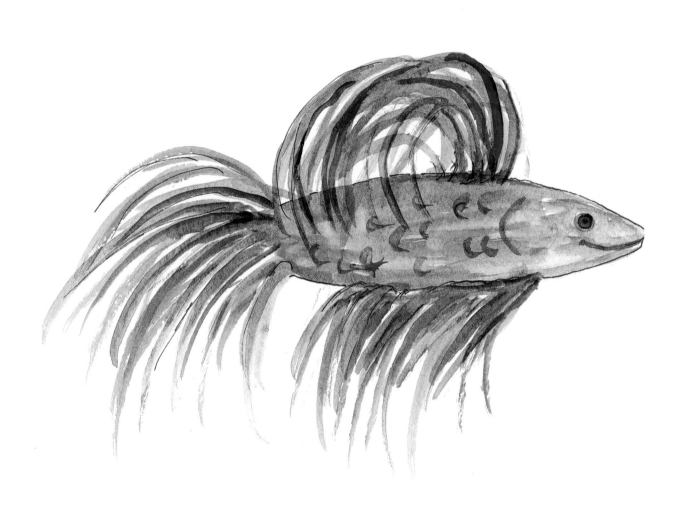

DADDY'S EGO

My Daddy got an ego.
I want to get one too.
Mommy says that his is swollen,
But I want one that's new.

He didn't get a good one.
It's not feeling very well.
Swollen things are broken,
That's how I can tell.

I've never seen his ego,
But it's up there on his shelf.
Inside the bowling trophy
That my daddy won himself.

THE GUPPY

My brother got a dog.
I just got some fish.
So I put a guppy
In the puppy's water dish.

But the puppy didn't like that.
He bit off the guppy's head.
Now my brother is responsible
That my favorite fish is dead.

So I offered him a trade,
As fair as he could wish,
That tiny newborn puppy,
For both pieces of my fish.

But my brother wouldn't do it.
He even tried to spoil it.
He took my favorite little fish,
And flushed him down the toilet.

MY BICYCLE

I built myself a bicycle,
The wheels turned out square.
You may think it would bother me,
But really, I don't care.

It makes lots of noise when you ride it,
The front wheel really thumps.
But the road can be awfully rocky,
And you don't even notice the bumps.